A Children's Book About

THROWING TANTRUMS

Managing Editor: Ellen Klarberg
Copy Editor: Annette Gooch
Editorial Assistant: Lana Eberhard
Art Director: Jennifer Wiezel
Production Artist: Gail Miller
Illustration Designer: Bartholomew
Inking Artist: Micah Schwaberow
Coloring Artists: Barbara Baird, Susie Hornig
Lettering Artist: Linda Hanney
Typographer: Communication Graphics

A Children's Book About

THROWING TANTRUMS

By Joy Berry

GROLIER ENTERPRISES CORP.

This book is about Annie and her friend Tami.

Reading about Annie and Tami can help you understand and deal with **throwing tantrums.**

You are throwing a tantrum when you show
your anger loudly and violently. A tantrum
is an outburst of bad temper or anger.

You might become angry if *people do not do what you want*. You might want to throw a tantrum.

You might become angry if *you must do something you do not want to do.* You might want to throw a tantrum.

You might become angry if *you cannot have something you want*. You might want to throw a tantrum.

You might become angry if *things do not happen the way you want them to happen.* You might want to throw a tantrum.

You might hurt yourself or others if you throw a tantrum.

You might ruin something if you throw a tantrum.

You might bother the people around you if you throw a tantrum. They might decide they do not want to be around you.

When you are angry, you should never do anything to hurt yourself or others. You should not do anything that would damage or destroy things.

This does not mean you should not get angry. It does not mean you should keep angry feelings to yourself.

When you are angry, you might need to do something to express your angry feelings.

You might want to express your anger by crying, yelling, jumping up and down, or hitting things (such as pillows, punching bags, or mattresses). It is OK to do these things as long as you do not disturb other people or damage or destroy anything.

To avoid disturbing others, you might need to go outside or into another room while you express your anger. You might need to go someplace away from other people until you calm down.

Talk with someone after you calm down. The best person to talk with is the person who made you angry.

If you cannot talk with that person, talk with someone else. Tell the person how you feel and why you feel angry.

Try to decide how you should handle your anger. Think of what you could do to make things better.

Do what you have decided to do. Then avoid doing things that make you or other people angry.

It is important that you express your anger without throwing a tantrum.

You and the people around you will be happier when you deal with your anger properly.

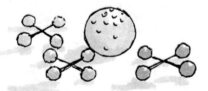